ISBN:978-1-4251-7195-7

*We at Trafford believe that it is the responsibility of us all, as both individuals
and corporations, to make choices that are environmentally and socially sound.
You, in turn, are supporting this responsible conduct each time you purchase a
Trafford book, or make use of our publishing services. To find out how you are
helping, please visit www.trafford.com/responsiblepublishing.html*

*Our mission is to efficiently provide the world's finest, most comprehensive
book publishing service, enabling every author to experience success.
To find out how to publish your book, your way, and have it available
worldwide, visit us online at www.trafford.com/10510*

www.trafford.com

North America & international
toll-free: 1 888 232 4444 (USA & Canada)
phone: 250 383 6864 ♦ fax: 250 383 6804
email: info@trafford.com

The United Kingdom & Europe
phone: +44 (0)1865 487 395 ♦ local rate: 0845 230 9601
facsimile: +44 (0)1865 481 507 ♦ mail: info.uk@trafford.com

10 9 8 7 6 5 4 3 2

Acknowledgements

To my mother for the gift of writing, laughing and sharing.

Many thanks to Martin for being my muse. Without him, this book would not have been produced.

To Pierre Perreault for the beautiful photos and his kind friendship.

To Carole Trépanier for translating my story and for her encouraging words.

To Dominique Viau, for the illustrations, the designs and the endless support.

Thank you.

Dedication

To all the Adjanis and Mareks of the world who keep the memories of Jesus' birth alive and vivid. Regardless of age, ethnicity, gender or status, these Collectors of Nativity scenes, or crèches, are greatly appreciated throughout the world for nourishing our hopes and dreams of a better place – one filled with peace, harmony and serenity.

Prologue

Years ago, there was a little boy who started collecting miniature Nativity scenes from all around the world. Once people knew he was collecting them, they began giving them to him as gifts. He received several new Nativity scenes every single year. His name is Jean Y. Lafond. Jean now has over 100 Nativity scenes in his collection, and he is still receiving new ones, some quite unique, every year at Christmas time. Among those who have given Jean Nativity scenes is his sister Ginette Lafond. Together, Jean and Ginette have decided to write this captivating story to highlight the reasons why so many people collect Nativity scenes, also known as "crèches".

Country of origin: Burkina Faso, Africa
Material: batik

Country of origin: Bengladesh
Material: ceramic

The child had been hearing noises coming from his neighbour's house for a few days. He didn't know his new neighbour yet, as the child had just moved to the small village of Nazareth. Every evening, the child heard the man toiling away in his workshop. He decided to go next door and satisfy his curiosity.

Through the half-opened door of the workshop, he saw his new neighbour—hunched over, concentrating, and handling a few pieces of wood. In his hands he held a hammer; a saw and a plane were nearby. His feet were covered with shavings which he seemed to have carefully piled under the bench. The child watched him work, but didn't dare approach, for fear of disturbing him. Finally he entered, and the man welcomed him with a warm smile and sparkling eyes.

Country of origin: Ontario, Canada
Material: wood

"Hello! What's your name?" said the man.

"Marek. I'm your new neighbour."

Suddenly, through the open door, the man spotted a shooting star speeding across the night sky. He was startled and amazed. Seeing a shooting star was a completely new experience for him, though he'd been awaiting that very moment for years.

"I am pleased to make your acquaintance, Marek, and welcome to Nazareth. My name is Adjani."

Country of origin: Colombia
Materials: stone, terra-cotta, wood

Marek asked him what he was doing.

"I carve Nativity scenes," replied Adjani.

"Why?" asked Marek.

"Let me tell you a story. It is a memorable experience which I lived when I was very young--hardly older than you are now. Do you want to hear it?"

"Of course!" exclaimed Marek, very intrigued.

Country of origin: England
Material: cloth

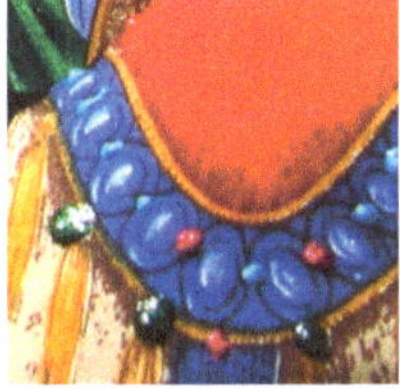

After having set aside his work and tools, Adjani sat on a bench and began. "The events were so long ago that you would think I would have forgotten this story, but even though it took place many moons ago, it remains crystal clear--so extraordinary a story it is!"

"One evening, I sat daydreaming in the grass under the moonlight. My eyes wide and a smile on my face, I was watching my sheep and thinking of all the good things happening in my life. In spite of my mere ten years, I'd already started to feel like a man; I worked from morning 'til night--like my father. He worked in the city when the field work was done and the animals were content. My mother was also very busy with my two little brothers, Nadiv and Sagui--three year old twins. We were all very happy together, and after supper, I would spend some time with my father in his workshop while my mother looked after the twins.

Country of origin: Indonesia
Material: metal

"My father adored carving and crafting toys for my little brothers. For the previous few months, he'd been letting me help him more and more. For the previous few weeks, when I was at the house, I'd been doing most of the work, under my father's watchful eye. He'd often tell me that I was a quick learner, and his compliments motivated me to improve the quality of my work. Every evening, my father brought home pieces of wood and metal which were no longer useful to him in his work in the city. With these, I would make toys for the twins--who appreciated my efforts, as did my parents who were very proud of me.

Country of origin: Ireland
Material: porcelain

Every day, from morning to evening, I would watch the sheep in a field far away from the house. Sometimes, I even had to sleep outside under the stars, far from my family. After a few days, I would return home with the flock, happy to be there and grateful to have such a loving family. I was always glad to return so I could see my younger brothers and tell them of my adventures before they went off to bed. Then, I'd have a peaceful evening with my parents before I too went to sleep in my warm, comfortable bed. We are so comfy in our own bed!

Country of origin: Norway
Materials: moss, plastic, wood

"That night--it was towards the end of December--while squatting in the grass and playing melodic tunes on my flute to put my sheep to sleep, I noticed a strange and bright light that rose to a fixed point in the sky, about an hour's walk away. I also heard a soft harmonious song emanating from the same point. I wanted to get a closer look at the light, but already my sheep were at rest and most were fast asleep. I was content then to lie down too and get some sleep, lulled by the enchanted music. Beside me slept Frizz, my favourite little lamb. She was always at my side.

Country of origin: Peru
Material: terra-cotta

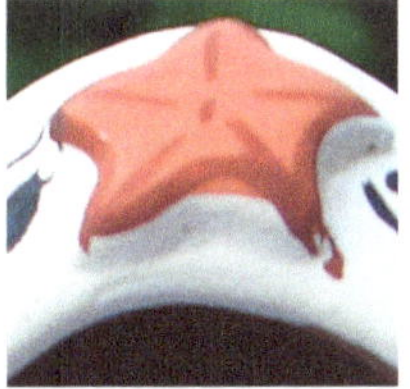

"The next morning, I awoke to the songs of the birds. I adore waking to the sounds of nature. Sometimes, it's the water from the river which pulls me from my dreams, while at other times, it's the wind in the leaves. When I must sleep outside, I truly feel my place in nature, as I'm awakened by it at the same time as it. On that day, nature's song was unlike anything I'd ever heard before. Wide-eyed and turning my head to hear it more clearly, the song, which was coming from the tree behind me, was almost unbelievable. I saw a bird with white feathers, which was not at all afraid of my presence. It even seemed happy to see me, coming closer as it hopped from branch to branch and sang louder and louder. For several minutes I remained lounging, still, watching it with amazement, speaking softly to it and praising its vocal talents.

Country of origin: Dominican Republic
Material: terra-cotta

"The bird sang, and I was somehow capable of understanding all of the song's lyrics. Once again I was reminded of how vital it is to listen to all the sounds that surround us, as they almost always bring important messages to us. With a soft and melodious voice, the bird told me that a very special child was born that night. It added that my visit, and all that I'd bring, would make the child very happy. In the chorus, which it repeated often, the bird invited me to follow it all the way to where the child was resting, to pay homage to Him. The bird sang and spoke, and I continued to listen. I was completely mesmerized by the glow and richness of its pure white plumage, and I was enchanted by the beauty of all that came from its beak—especially the messages of love and peace. After a few minutes, I decided to follow it.

Country of origin: Vietnam
Materials: soapstone, straw, wood

"Still singing, the bird hopped from one tree to another, waiting for me to arrive with my flock. My sheep followed my orders well on that day, as we were moving towards new pastures. My heart was filled with joy! These kinds of surprising and unexpected adventures cut the monotony which is far too common in the life of shepherds. Lost in my thoughts of the newborn child, I noticed only at the last minute that we found ourselves, almost like magic, in a field of flowers which I never knew existed—a field filled with thousands of scarlet red flowers. Again it was pure fantasy, as I'd just thought of how lovely it would be to bring a present to the newborn child's parents.

Country of origin: Bethlehem, West Bank
Material: olive tree

"While picking several flowers and placing them in my sac, I kept an eye on my flock. I then guided them, at the bird's invitation, to a forgotten place which my mother had once described to me. Her parents lived in a little house which was now abandoned and in ruins. Only a stable remained—witness to the place where once lived my maternal grandparents and my mother. Despite the fact that the stable now belonged to my parents, they would rarely go, as they knew that the neighbouring fields could no longer provide nutrition to our animals. These rocky lands were not as valuable as the rich clay fields where the grass grew for our sheep.

Country of origin: Canada
Material: plastic

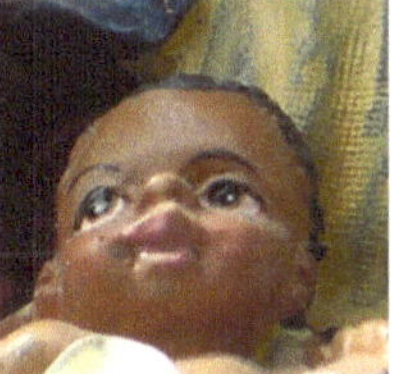

"As I neared the area, I saw that the right side of the house had collapsed under its own weight, but that the stable still seemed solid. Peace reigned there. Only the murmur of the townsfolk and the barking of local dogs broke the calm which hung over the place.

"Once close to the stable, I was stunned to see that it was inhabited. Hiding behind an olive tree, I could make out three people. A child, wrapped in swaddling blankets, was lying on hay in a manger. Before Him were two animals—a bull and a donkey. The mother was busy preparing a meal a little ways away, while a man was cutting branches for the cooking fire. The child seemed to sleep under the bull's and donkey's warm breath.

Country of origin: Canada
Material: plasticine

"The bird continued its melodious song and invited me again to follow it to the newborn. Only a few feet from the manger, I attentively watched the baby. He then opened His eyes wide and fixed them onto me. Approaching the child, I gave Him my first gift, a simple little gift, the only one I had in my hands—a small piece of wood I'd begun to carve for my two brothers. I knew that all little boys liked playing with small pieces of wood. My gesture made the child smile and He reached His hand out to me, under the approving gaze of the bird. It began to sing even more beautifully—which seemed to fascinate the child.

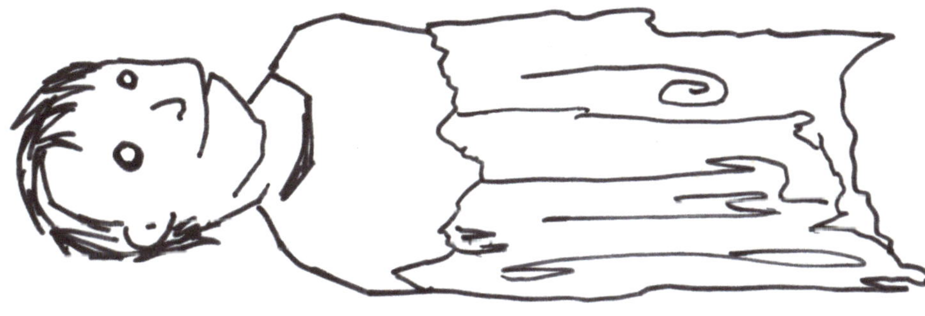

Country of origin: Mexico
Materials: clay, wood

"My flock remained on the other side of the olive tree, grazing peacefully. Only two lambs, Frizz and Blacky, followed me to the manger, where they settled close to eat. Whereas Blacky lay on the ground, Frizz remained upright, and the child succeeded in touching Frizz's muzzle, under the watchful eye of the bull. The child and Frizz looked attentively at each other, and even seemed to speak, so enthralled they were by one another. Then the mother approached us. Peace emanated from her entire being. In a soft voice, perhaps even angelic, she asked me my name.

'Adjani,' I said to her.

'I am Mary. Over there is Joseph, my husband.'

Country of origin: Mexico
Materials: clay, glass, walnut

"She then introduced me to Jesus, and after petting the two lambs and smiling at the bird, she left to continue preparing the meal a few steps from the manger.

"During the moments shared with Jesus, I was unable to avert my eyes. He was not the first tiny baby I'd seen, but I was hypnotized by the beauty of His face—especially the vividness and gleam of His eyes. I took the flowers out of my sac, and laid them at His feet. Mary, His mother, turned and smiled at me, and the child let out a squeal of joy.

Country of origin: Canada
Material: egg

"I had to leave a little while later, as my animals were waiting, but I promised to return the following day. The moment I made that decision, Jesus' eyes sparkled and He smiled at me. It was as though He had read my thoughts!

"I gathered my flock and decided to leave behind my two lambs until my return the following day. I felt that their presence near Jesus, especially Frizz who remained close to Him, would help Him stay warm in His manger.

Country of origin: Peru
Material: terra-cotta

"In the following days, I returned to the stable every afternoon. I spent nearly all my time with Jesus, exchanging only a few words with the parents who, nevertheless, were very happy to see me and give me a little food. I could never stay very long, given that my animals needed to drink in the river and graze along the bank. I noticed that Frizz and the white bird were extremely loyal to their stations. Frizz remained standing close to Jesus, while the bird, perched on one of the stable's beams, continued to entertain Him with its melodic songs.

Country of origin: Mexico
Material: clay

"Then one afternoon I returned and couldn't believe my eyes! The stable was empty! Jesus was gone! Mary was gone! Joseph was gone! The bull and donkey were gone!

"Only my two lambs awaited me, and they seemed very happy to see me. On my knees, I comforted them while looking around. The cooking fire had been doused, there was no longer hay in the manger, and the white bird had disappeared. An eerie silence reigned. Only the sound of my beating heart, quickened by the deception, broke the silence which had infiltrated there. Crushed, I realized that I would miss the child and the daily visits which I had always looked forward to. My head hung low and my feet heavy, I returned to my animals and led them to the river, where I sat and wallowed in my grief. Sensing my sadness, Frizz lay next to me, resting her head on my thigh. My only glimmer of happiness was in the fact that I was returning to my home that evening with the animals. Home--where I could spend time with my family. I especially looked forward to giving two new carvings I'd made to my brothers.

Country of origin: Peru
Material: clay

"After a brief stay at my home, I returned to the same stable, expecting to see Jesus and His parents. But, alas, it was in vain. They were gone forever. A tear in my eye, I left the stable. I held with me the beautiful memories of the days I spent in their company.

"Over the next few months, I would occasionally pass by the stable with my flock. Always, the place was devoid of life. Always, the place was silent. It seemed that even the grass, flowers and birds had left the area. Only Frizz seemed to become more animated and excited when near the stable.

Country of origin: Canada
Material: metal

"The story continues twelve years later. At the age of 22, I'd already left the house and the country to work in the city. Like my father, I'd become a jack-of-all-trades. I could build houses, fix furniture, and forge metal. I was now skilled at all types of work.

"One day, I had to go to Jerusalem to help my uncle and my cousins build a house and repair the furnishings in the Temple. Soon we would be celebrating Passover, and the entire village was preparing for the occasion. It was the first time that I'd been to Jerusalem, and I felt that my brief time there would change my life forever.

Country of origin: Peru
Material: stone

"In fact, three days later, while I was busily repairing the benches in the Temple, I saw a young man of about 12 years of age enter. He was carrying an object in His hand which He placed on a bench I'd previously repaired and moved near the incense burners. Then He turned, smiled, nodded His head and said, 'It's for you. It is a gift for you, in appreciation of all that you do. It is a gift for you, in appreciation of all that you WILL do.'

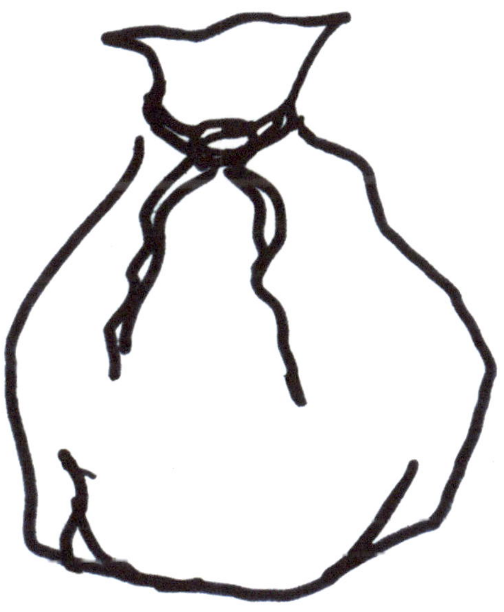

Country of origin: Canada
Material: plastic

"He locked eyes with me, smiled, and after a long and intense moment, He made His way to the group of Teachers who were sitting on the benches in the center of the Temple. It was then that I recognized Him…Jesus!

"Trembling with joy, I picked up the small gift and watched Jesus discourse with the Teachers. For three hours, He answered their questions and allayed their concerns. Completely at ease, He stood in the center of the group, captivating them with His words. Never had I ever seen anything like it!

Country of origin: Canada
Material: plastic

"Without shyness, He spoke openly and freely about love, peace, wisdom, responsibility, respect and faith. When He spoke of family, of relations, of growth and divinity the Teachers watched their mouths agape. It was in that moment that I recognized that He was very special, this Jesus!

"Given that I'd promised to meet my uncle near the village well, I left the Temple, completely enchanted by the lovely surprise and clutching my gift. Jesus stayed at the Temple with the Teachers who spoke, listened, questioned, responded, and showed approval with nodding heads.

Country of origin: Canada
Material: wood

"That evening, alone in my room, I studied at length the gift from Jesus. Upon closer examination of the gift, my mind was awhirl with thoughts. It was then that I recognized it! It was the piece of wood that I'd given Him at His birth, in the stable! With His own hands, a good decade later, He had continued to carve it and had created a tiny figurine of a shepherd. Stunned, completely touched by the surprise meeting with Jesus, and humbled by the simplicity of His gesture, I placed the figurine on the table near my bed and fell asleep, smile on lips, serene despite the exhaustion.

Country of origin: Canada
Material: plastic

 "A few days later, I returned to Nazareth to visit and help out my parents for a few weeks. One morning, I decided to care for the sheep and lead them to the river, which was quite far away. I knew that I would have to sleep beneath the stars as I did when I was younger, but I also felt I would benefit from this time of solitude.

Country of origin: Canada
Material: metal

"That afternoon, when the sun hid behind the clouds, I walked with my flock near the stable where Jesus was born. Confident that all my animals were near enough to the river, I decided to move closer to the stable. I soon noticed that the stable had rapidly deteriorated. A structure which was still very solid just a few years ago, the stable had now become dilapidated. I saw it now on the ground, as run-down as the house. I had a difficult time accepting that this place was now in ruins. I decided to fill my sac with the wood of the stable, and to create a small Nativity scene with it when I next returned home.

Country of origin: Dominican Republic
Material: terra-cotta

"That very evening, I sat on the ground in front of my small campfire, under the sparkling stars, playing a melancholic air on my flute. All the sheep slept peacefully. Only Frizz, who had now become a beautiful ewe, stayed awake. She moved closer to the crackling fire, lay next to me and rested her head on my thigh.

"Petting her head, I spoke to her about everything and nothing, and told her of my adventure at the Temple, of my meeting with Jesus and of the reaction of the Teachers to His words. I also showed her the present Jesus had given me—the shepherd figurine. I also spoke of my decision to carve a little nativity scene. For me, it was important to build it, because I didn't want to forget the birth of Jesus, a child who had become an eloquent, fascinating and extraordinary young man.

Country of origin: Germany
Material: plaster

"At this moment, Frizz got up and stood a few feet in front of me. She looked at me attentively and intensely, and uttered a few short bleating sounds. Then, we lay side by side, and attempted to sleep under the canopy of stars. Every now and again, I would whistle a familiar tune, and Frizz would bleat. It was a type of dialogue between us. Little by little, our eyelids grew heavy and sleep succeeded at taming us.

Country of origin: Mexico
Material: plaster

"The next morning, I awoke completely rested. All night I'd dreamt of angels, stars, shepherds, kings, sheep, Mary, Joseph and, of course, of Jesus who spoke frequently to me. In my dreams, I spoke at length with Jesus, and His words still ring clear in my mind.

"He began by thanking me for the gifts received at His birth: the songs of the white bird, the company of Frizz and Blacky during His stay in the stable, the flowers that I'd placed at His feet, and the piece of wood that I'd begun to carve. All these gifts had been greatly appreciated.

Country of origin: Mexico
Material: plasticine

"Then, He spoke to me about the white bird and its messages of love and peace. He told me that at times, men would forget the importance of mutual understanding, but that henceforth, they would always remember the goodness of peace, tranquility, calm and serenity when they saw the bird of peace.

Country of origin: Cuba
Material: plaster

"Afterwards, He thanked me for Frizz's presence, which had been His first contact with the external world, except for His parents. The moment she'd entered the stable, Frizz had moved towards the manger, and remained standing nearly all hours of the day and night. When He touched her muzzle with His tiny hand, Jesus spoke to her and thanked her profusely for her presence. In return, she felt His warm human compassion, and His messages of appreciation, peace and love.

"Each night, Frizz had warmed Jesus with her breath. Her own exhaustion aside, she'd taken her role seriously, making use of her body heat for the benefit of the child Jesus. Ah, how a gesture as simple as a breath can make all the difference to someone's life! Frizz's breath, along with that of her brother Blacky, the bull and the donkey had offered Jesus warmth, and comfortable, restful nights.

Country of origin: Poland
Materials: plaster, wood

"The flowers that I'd left had also greatly touched Jesus and His mother Mary. The red flowers brought colour to the stable and to His mother's anxious heart. Henceforth, announced Jesus in my dream, all mothers of the Earth would appreciate this simple loving gesture--one which says so very much.

Country of origin: Canada
Material: glass

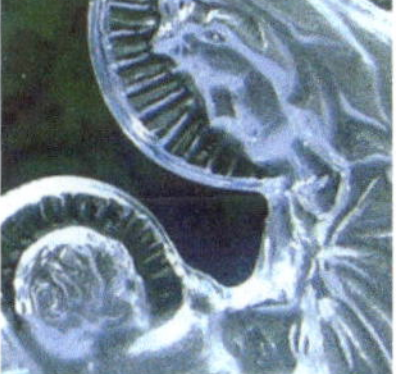

"Jesus also told me just how happy He was to receive the tiny piece of wood. His very first toy! You rarely forget your first toy! This one had brought Him much joy during His first years, and once He was a little older, He had succeeded in transforming it with His father's help--in giving it a little life. He said that this same object would one day be a source of great inspiration to me--the young man who had been the first on Earth to show Jesus the great value of gifts.

Country of origin: Sri Lanka
Material: terra-cotta

"Then, He congratulated me on the beautiful work I'd done repairing the Temple benches. He told me how important it was to accept our talents and to use them for good ends. He made me understand that I must use my carpentry and forging talents as much as possible to help others—in the same way that my twin brothers must use their writing talents and their intelligence to guide and teach younger children how to read and write. To each his or her own gifts!

Country of origin: El Salvador
Material: terra-cotta

"Later in my dream, Jesus spoke of my decision to carve a small Nativity scene. He encouraged me to build as many as possible, and to distribute them to whoever might want one. He made me understand that if I built only one, and I placed it on the table in my room as I'd originally planned, very few people would view it and know of this very special night. The more people had Nativity scenes, the more people would experience, in their heart, the special nature of this night. He assured me that there would be stable wood available for this purpose as long as I wanted some. I would only need to continue using the pieces I'd placed in my sac, and Jesus would see to it that there would always be enough.

Country of origin: Peru
Material: soapstone

"While on the topic of Nativity scenes, Jesus mentioned an important point. He made me realize that in His Nativity scene, with Him were Mary and Joseph, the animals, the shepherds, the Wise Men, and even angels sent from heaven. He therefore invited me to include, whenever possible, all these characters in my Nativity scenes. This way, all who would see my Nativity scenes would observe that it is possible to bring together the richest, the poorest, the youngest and the oldest.

Country of origin: Mexico
Materials: cotton, straw, wood

"He also spoke to me of the people who would become collectors of Nativity scenes. Thanks to the collectors' exhibitions, more and more people throughout the ages would come to know the story of Jesus' birth. Some of these would carve and build these Nativity scenes, but in general, most would be content to accumulate them.

"Despite that fact that there would be many collectors, there would only be one Great Collector per country. The role of these Great Collectors would be to ensure that the Nativity scene's significance be known by as many people as possible. Through their devotion to this cause, and their wisdom and knowledge, these Great Collectors would see that other children would come to know and experience the world of Nativity scenes.

Country of origin: Peru
Materials: egg, plaster

"It is easy to know which country requires a Great Collector. In the sky, there will be a shooting star which will announce to the world the need for another Great Collector. This star will remind people to reflect on the beauty of all that surrounds them, on their role in the world, and the similarities of the peoples of the world, regardless of race.

Country of origin: El Salvador
Material: terra-cotta

"Given that I'd never seen a shooting star before and didn't really know what they were, Jesus explained them to me in His own words:

Shooting stars are fragments of the Great Star which guided the Wise Men the night of my birth. These bits of the Great Star will travel the skies until the end of time, inspiring men to stop and observe the celestial wonders, to think, ponder, marvel and dream. Never will a shooting star go unnoticed. To those who observe it carefully, it will bring wonder, curiosity, hope and peace. Henceforth, shooting stars will join the rest of the beautiful celestial bodies already in existence, and will form an integral part of our Universe. As opposed to the many other aspects of nature which we admire, shooting stars will be remarkable for their actions, and not for their beauty alone.

"He ended His lesson on shooting stars by telling me that I would see one, for the very first time, once I was in the presence of the first Great Collector of Nativity scenes.

Country of origin: Portugal
Materials: metal, wood

"So that, Marek, is why I make Nativity scenes. Without them, the story of Jesus' birth may go unnoticed. Since the night that Jesus came to speak to me in my dreams, I have crafted, over time, nearly forty different Nativity scenes using shells, metal, wood, straw and shavings. I have always been able to integrate a piece of wood from the stable where Jesus was born, and I still have some left. I can therefore continue building Nativity scenes. If it is of interest to you, Marek, you could come help me in the evening, after our daily activities and dinner."

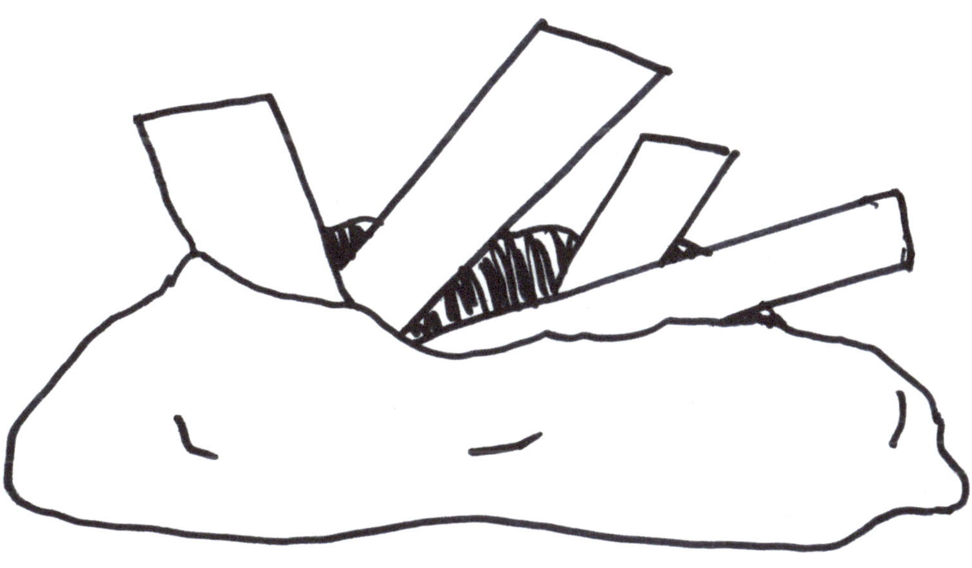

Country of origin: Peru
Materials: cardboard, plastic

 And so it was, that from that night forward, Marek and Adjani crafted Nativity scenes and distributed them to those interested—a question of paying homage to Jesus, and a question of ensuring that His story would never be forgotten. Every now and again, they would look into the night sky, just in case they might catch a glimpse of a shooting star. You never know!

Country of origin: El Salvador
Material: terra-cotta

 Every night, even when Marek was unable to join him, Adjani continued to toil in his workshop. Little by little, he began sharing his Nativity scenes with Marek. Giving him the Nativity scenes felt right, as he knew that Marek understood the story, the sacredness of the story, and the special nature of the story of Jesus' birth. He knew that his Nativity scenes were in good hands. He knew that Marek would take on the responsibility of sharing them with others. He knew that because of the world's collectors of Nativity scenes, especially the Great Collectors, the story would live on.

Country of origin: Canada
Material: acrylic

One day, 21 years after his decision to craft Nativity scenes, Adjani used the last piece of wood from the stable. He could now rest. He could now think of the words uttered by Frizz and Marek.

"Thank you, Adjani, for the Nativity scenes. Thanks to you, the world will remember the most remarkable of stories. With time, these Nativity scenes will be called Crèches."

In fact, thanks to Adjani and the Great Collectors of Nativity scenes, or crèches, the story will never be forgotten.

Country of origin: Canada
Material: plastic

Country of origin: Mexico
Material: plastic

Country of origin: Canada
Materials: glass, plastic